FED UP!

D0545487

99p

50p

For Anita

This edition published in 1999 by Diamond Books
77-85 Fulham Palace Road,
Hammersmith, London, W6 8JB

First published in Great Britain by HarperCollins in 1991
First published in Picture Lions in 1993

Picture Lions is an imprint of the Children's Division,
part of HarperCollins Publishers Limited,
77-85 Fulham Palace Road, Hammersmith,
London W6 8JB

Text and illustrations copyright © Dennis Reader 1991

The author/illustrator asserts the moral right to be
identified as the author/illustrator of the work.

ISBN 0 261 67370 X

Printed and bound in Singapore by Tien Wah Press

This book is set in 18/23 New Baskerville

FED UP!

Dennis Reader

"I'm fed up!" said Anthony Anthony to his mother.

"What's the problem?" asked his mother.

"I'm fed up!" said Anthony Anthony.

"Go and play," said his mother. "Go and play on the adventure frame in the garden."

"I'm fed up!" said Anthony Anthony to his father.
"What is it this time?" asked his father.

"I'm fed up!" said Anthony Anthony.
"Go and play," said his father. "Get out your
skateboard and go to the skateboard park."

"I'm fed up!" said Anthony Anthony to his grandfather.

"There are always things to do," said his grandfather.
"Exciting things. Worthwhile things. Go and save
the rain forests."

"All right," said Anthony Anthony.

"I'm fed up again," said Anthony Anthony (just back from saving the rain forests) to his grandfather.

"Go and mend the hole in the ozone layer," said
his grandfather. "That's an interesting project."
"All right," said Anthony Anthony.

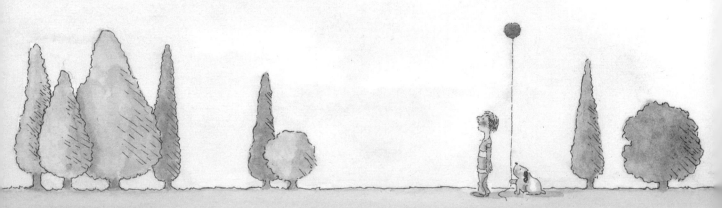

"I'm a little bit fed up," said Anthony Anthony (just back from
mending the hole in the ozone layer) to his grandfather.

"Go and save the whale," said his grandfather.
"That's worthwhile."
"All right," said Anthony Anthony.

"I'm still fed up," said Anthony Anthony (just back from saving the whale) to his grandfather.

"Go and save the world from the horrors of pollution," said his grandfather. "It's time someone did."

"All right," said Anthony Anthony.

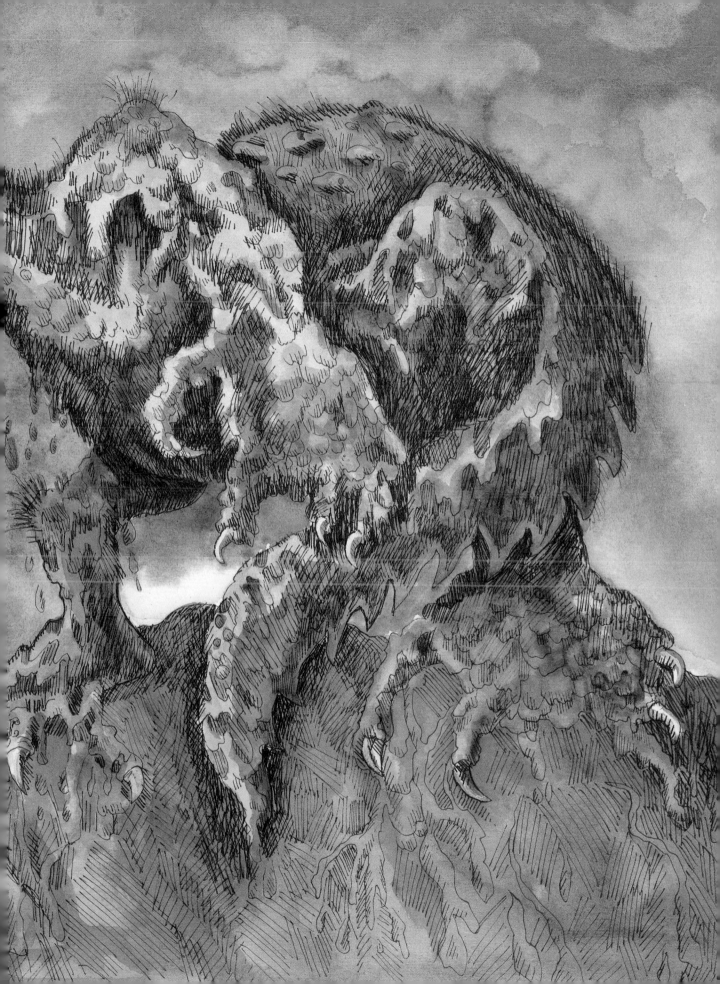

"How are we today?" said Anthony Anthony's grandfather.

"I feel fine today," said Anthony Anthony (just back from saving the world from the horrors of pollution) to his grandfather.

"You feel fine because you've been doing lots of interesting things," said Anthony Anthony's grandfather.

"There's plenty left to do," said Anthony Anthony. "There's elephants, for instance ..."

Mr and Mrs Anthony were having tea and biscuits
with Mr and Mrs Brown and their son Bramwell
from next door. Bramwell had painted a daffodil
of which Mr and Mrs Brown were very proud.
  "Gorgeous!" said Mr and Mrs Anthony. "So talented!"
  "Does your Anthony do anything?" asked Mrs Brown.

  "Nothing much," said Anthony Anthony's father.
"Climbs the adventure frame, skateboards a bit ..."

Dennis Reader was born in Peterborough in 1930. He learnt to draw at art evening classes – which cost him nine old pennies for two hours! Dennis did not become a full time illustrator until the late eighties when his first book, BEN AND THE AMAZING POT PLANT (written by Diana Webb) was published. This was followed by a further two titles – A LOVELY BUNCH OF COCONUTS and I WANT ONE.

Other titles by Dennis Reader published by
HarperCollins:
BUTTERFINGERS
JOE USELESS